PINOCCHIO

DERRYDALE BOOKS
New York

A division of Crown Publishers, Inc.
New York

© Award Publications Ltd. MCMLXXX
Spring House, Spring Place
London NW5, England.

Library of Congress Catalog Card Number : 79-13751

This edition is published by Derrydale Books, a division
of Crown Publishers, Inc., One Park Avenue
New York, New York 10016

a b c d e f g h
Printed in Belgium.

Once upon a time there was... a piece of wood! It was found by a carpenter, who soon realized that this was no ordinary piece of wood, for he felt sure it was alive! Knowing his old friend Gepetto was lonely (and being rather frightened of it himself!) he gave the wood to Gepetto who hurried home and began to carve it.

His plan was to make a puppet, but as he carved, the wood seemed to change by itself until, in no time at all, there was a mischievous looking wooden boy staring at him from the workbench. Suddenly it stood up, seized Gepetto's wig from his bald head — and ran off laughing!

Pinocchio (for this was the name Gepetto gave him) was never out of trouble. He teased poor old Gepetto by day and by night, hiding his tools, spilling his glue and mixing paint with his porridge! He was much, much naughtier than you or I have *ever* been and nothing Gepetto said seemed to make him better.
When the wise little Cricket who lived on the wall tried to tell Pinocchio to be good and think about going to school, that horrid puppet threw Gepetto's hammer at him!

Pinocchio thought about the Cricket's sensible words that night and decided he would try to be good. When he told Gepetto that he wanted to go to school, the kind old man, who was very poor, sold his only coat to buy books for Pinocchio. But on the way to school the first day, Pinocchio saw a puppet theater and, without a second thought, sold his new schoolbooks to buy a ticket for the show.

The Cricket, who had followed Pinocchio just in case he thought about being naughty again, shouted "No! No!" as loudly as he could, but Pinocchio pretended not to hear him.

Inside the theater Pinocchio was amazed to see
that the actors, like him, were made from wood,
although they were moved by strings. Pinocchio
was so excited he pushed to the front of the
audience and climbed onto the stage.

When the puppets' owner heard the audience boo-ing and demanding their money back he was very angry and, closing the curtains, he seized the nearest puppet by the collar and dragged him backstage. "You" he said in a terrible voice "are only fit for the fire!" and was about to drop him onto the blaze when Pinocchio stepped forward. "It w-was all m-my f-fault" he stammered. "It was I who spoiled the show. Please punish *me* if you must."

The puppets' owner was so amazed and delighted, for his
puppets spoke only the words they had been taught for the
performances, that his anger left him completely. Grinning
through his black beard he patted Pinocchio's wooden
head and gave him some gold pieces for his bravery.

When Pinocchio set off home, he jingled the gold in his
pocket and thought how he would spend it on a new
coat for Gepetto. On the way he met a Cat and a Fox
and all three walked along together. Towards evening,
when they were all tired and hungry, they came to an
Inn and decided to rest there and eat supper.

Perhaps they had heard the coins in Pinocchio's pocket, for both the Cat and the Fox ate enormous helpings of everything on the menu. Then, saying they needed to wash their paws and whiskers, they disappeared through a side door... leaving Pinocchio to pay!

Soon after leaving the Inn, Pinocchio, who could not believe that his new friends had deliberately tricked him, was pounced upon by two masked thieves. Despite their disguises Pinocchio thought he recognized the silky fur and hooked claws — and he held tightly onto what was left of his money.

Angry that their plan had failed, the robbers hung
Pinocchio from a high branch and left him there.
However, the tree was an old one: the dying branch
soon broke under Pinocchio's struggles and he fell to
the ground with a bump.

When he awoke
Pinocchio found himself in a
large, soft bed in a strange house. At the end of
the bed was a lovely Fairy with blue hair; she
had saved him and called the three best doctors
she knew to make him well. Doctors Owl, Crow
and Cricket all agreed that if he took his
medicine he would recover completely.

By this time, however, Pinocchio was feeling much better... and much naughtier! He threw the medicine bottle across the bed and stuck out his tongue at the kind doctors. The Fairy was very upset by his rude behaviour and explained that they were all trying to help him. She asked how he came to be lying under the tree (although, being a Fairy, she already knew!) and, when Pinocchio had finished his story, she asked him where he had hidden the remaining money. "Oh, it's *all* gone now" he lied.

Immediately the Fairy cast a spell to punish him, and his sharp wooden nose suddenly grew out from his face like a carrot!!

Pinocchio was furious! He jumped from the bed and ran around the room screaming, then kicked and rolled on the floor in a terrible tantrum! After several minutes Pinocchio saw that the Fairy was watching him sadly; seeing her kind face, he realized how foolish and wrong he had been. He hadn't meant to upset anyone — it just seemed much easier to be naughty than to be good!

Pinocchio sat up, quietly poured a spoonful of
medicine from the half-empty bottle and drank it
quickly. He then straightened the bed, tidied the
room and finally stood before the gentle Fairy.
"I'm sorry" he said humbly "I will *try* to behave
better."

The Fairy smiled and, as she did so,
Pinocchio's nose magically returned
to its proper size. Pinocchio thought how much
better he felt when he was
being good.

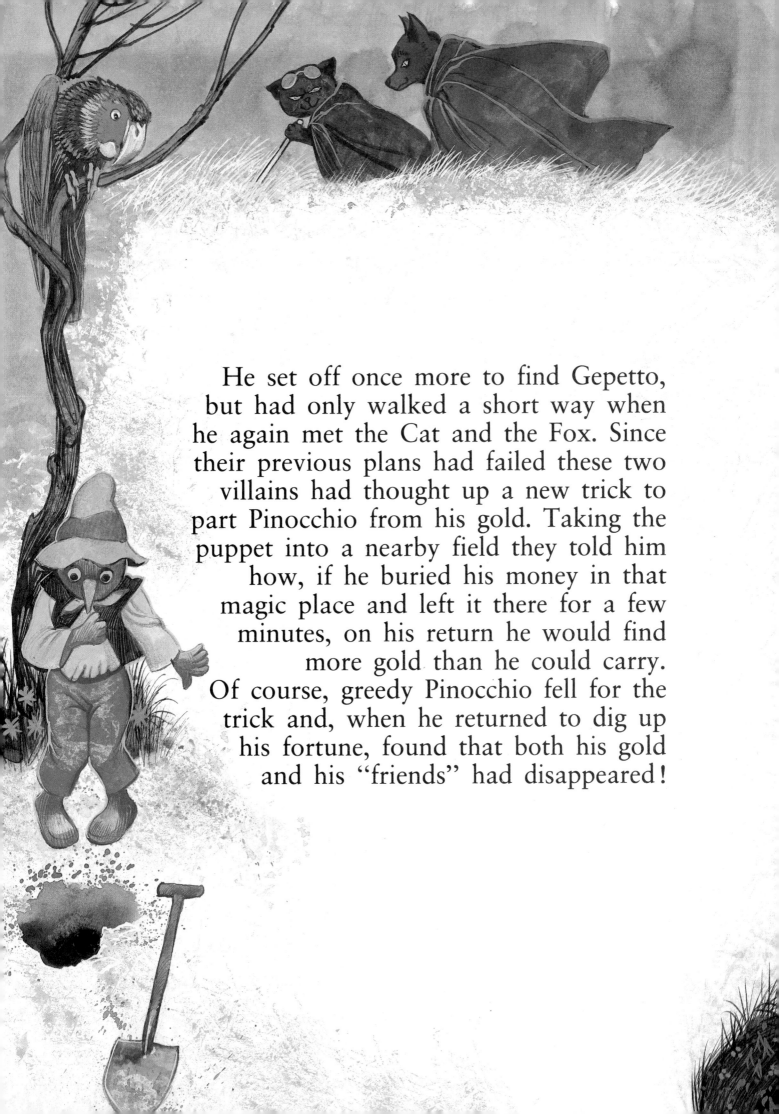

He set off once more to find Gepetto, but had only walked a short way when he again met the Cat and the Fox. Since their previous plans had failed these two villains had thought up a new trick to part Pinocchio from his gold. Taking the puppet into a nearby field they told him how, if he buried his money in that magic place and left it there for a few minutes, on his return he would find more gold than he could carry. Of course, greedy Pinocchio fell for the trick and, when he returned to dig up his fortune, found that both his gold and his "friends" had disappeared!

Penniless and alone, Pinocchio wandered for many months and had lots of adventures. He was thrown into prison, tricked by a giant snake, caught in a terrible trap and chained up as a farmer's watch-dog!

As time passed he felt less and less like being naughty — and he missed old Gepetto and the kind Fairy. At last he returned to the Fairy's house, having almost made up his mind to change his ways and become the sort of puppet they would like him to be.

As he hurried through her garden calling to his friend, Pinocchio came to a grave: on the headstone he read that it was the gentle Fairy who was buried there. Tears rolled down his wooden face and he cried "Why should you, who were so good and kind, have to die, while I, who am so wicked, do not?"

Now I will tell you that the Fairy was not dead, but was listening to Pinocchio to see if he really had changed his ways. When she heard his cries and saw the tears she came from her hiding place and called to him. You may imagine how overjoyed Pinocchio was to see her — (at first he thought she was a ghost!) — and he told her all his adventures since they last met.

"Do you see now how unkind you were?" asked the Fairy "and how your naughtiness hurt the people you love?"

"Oh I do" said Pinocchio "And if I promise you that I shall never again be so thoughtless and wicked, do you think that one day I may become a *real* boy?"

"That depends on you" replied the Fairy.

So Pinocchio started school, and for a while he worked hard and well. He stayed at his desk when the other boys were running about the playground and took no notice of their teasing. But, as the weeks passed, he longed to be out with them — they seemed to spend all their time playing games and having fun.

Pinocchio regarded one of these boys whose name was Candlewick as a special friend. He was the naughtiest and laziest boy in the school, but he always thought up the most exciting things to do.

One day Candlewick persuaded Pinocchio to go with him and his friends to the Land of Play where, he said, no one ever had to work or go to school.

"What a wonderful place" thought Pinocchio, and joined in all the games, pleasing himself from morning until night.

What neither he nor Candlewick realized was that without rules or work, without discipline or helping others, we all become stupid and selfish — and this is what happened to the puppet and his friends! At first they felt small, furry lumps on their heads: these grew into long, grey ears! Then their toes disappeared and in their place were hard, shiny hooves! Yes, you've guessed... they were all slowly turning into donkeys!!

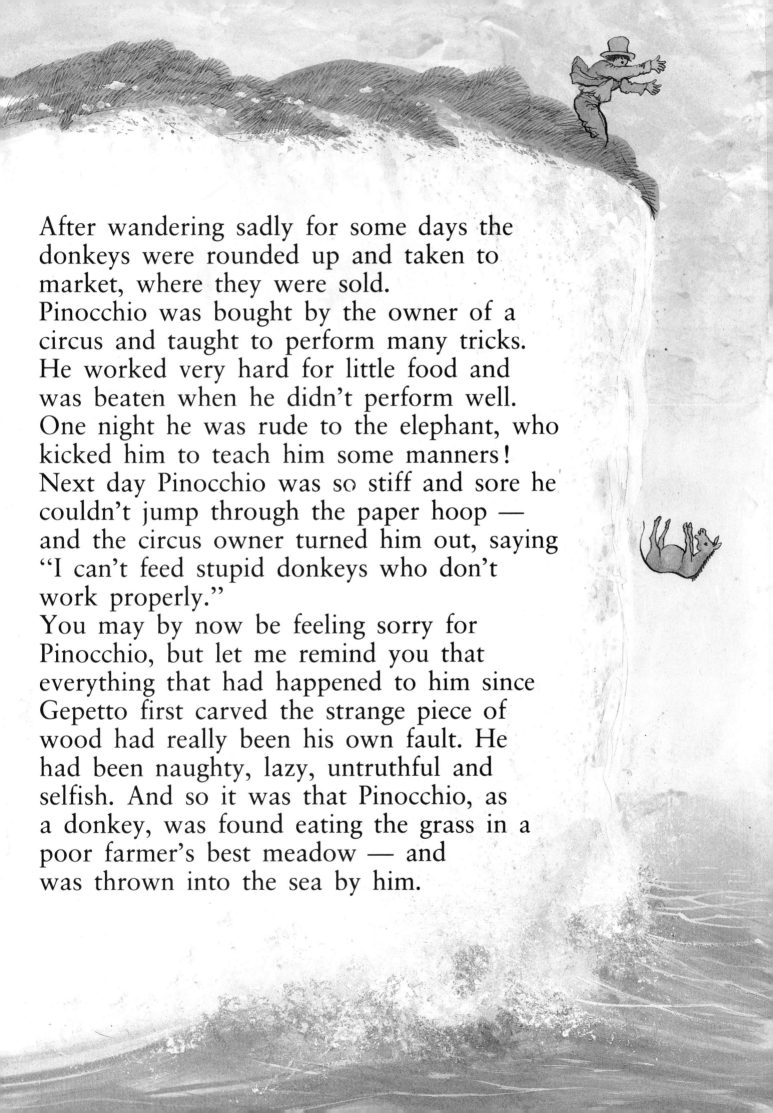

After wandering sadly for some days the donkeys were rounded up and taken to market, where they were sold.
Pinocchio was bought by the owner of a circus and taught to perform many tricks. He worked very hard for little food and was beaten when he didn't perform well. One night he was rude to the elephant, who kicked him to teach him some manners! Next day Pinocchio was so stiff and sore he couldn't jump through the paper hoop — and the circus owner turned him out, saying "I can't feed stupid donkeys who don't work properly."
You may by now be feeling sorry for Pinocchio, but let me remind you that everything that had happened to him since Gepetto first carved the strange piece of wood had really been his own fault. He had been naughty, lazy, untruthful and selfish. And so it was that Pinocchio, as a donkey, was found eating the grass in a poor farmer's best meadow — and was thrown into the sea by him.

But strangely, as Pinocchio hit the cold water, he felt himself changing back from a lame donkey into a wooden puppet. Looking over his shoulder, he saw with horror the tail-fin of a gigantic shark streaking towards him! Frantically he began to swim towards a rock, then noticed a curious animal standing on the rock. It was like a goat but with blue hair, just the color of the kind Fairy's hair. "Sweet Fairy" cried Pinocchio above the waves "Save me again!" As he neared the rock he saw the goat kneel down and lower her horns to help him, but just as he was about to pull himself out of the sea... SNAP!... all was dark!

When he recovered his breath Pinocchio tried to stand up: he could hear a distant roaring noise and the air was moist and fishy. When his eyes became used to the gloom he saw a faintly flickering light and, following it, who should he find inside the shark's belly but... Gepetto!

The old man was so pleased to see Pinocchio that he could hardly speak; he listened as the puppet told of all his adventures — of the puppet show, the Cat and the Fox, the dear Fairy, Candlewick, and how as a wretched donkey, he had been thrown into the sea to drown.

Hugging Pinocchio and laughing through his tears, old Gepetto told how he had built a small boat in order to search for the lost puppet, but during a storm the boat had sunk and the shark had swallowed him alive. When they had retold every adventure in detail and were both quite exhausted, Gepetto said "Now we must try to escape, for surely we shall not live for long in here, with no fresh air or water. Let's wait until the shark dozes on the surface in the afternoon sun — for he is old and snores with his mouth open!"

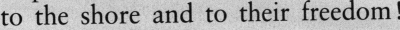

So they waited. Later that day they tiptoed along the monster's slippery tongue, climbed through his terrible teeth and jumped into the sea. Pinocchio took Gepetto on his back and swam strongly to the shore and to their freedom!